EFG
LMNOP
uVWXYZ

For Willie and Bo

IMPRINT
A part of Macmillan Publishing Group, LLC
175 Fifth Avenue, New York, NY 10010

ABOUT THIS BOOK
The art for this book was created with pen, ink, gouache, and watercolor. The text was set in ITC Cheltenham, and the display type is hand lettered. The book was edited by Erin Stein and designed by Natalie C. Sousa. The production was supervised by Raymond Ernesto Colón, and the production editor was Alexei Esikoff.

Printed in China by Toppan Leefung Printing Ltd., Dongguan City, Guangdong Province.

Our books may be purchased in bulk for promotional, educational, or business use.
Please contact your local bookseller or the Macmillan Corporate and
Premium Sales Department at (800) 221-7945 ext. 5442 or by
e-mail at MacmillanSpecialMarkets@macmillan.com.

Library of Congress Cataloging-in-Publication Data is available.

ISBN 978-1-250-12395-4

Imprint logo designed by Amanda Spielman

First Edition, 2018

10 9 8 7 6 5 4 3 2 1

mackids.com

X says, "Don't steal this book!
Unless you want a bunch of grumpy pirates
knocking on your door."

WRITTEN BY SEAN LAMB
ILLUSTRATED BY MIKE PERRY

Z GOES FIRST

[Imprint]
MAKE YOUR MARK
NEW YORK

ABC...

The letter Z was tired of being last in the alphabet. She wanted to go first.

A went first all the time. Like in "*a* puzzle" or "*a* pretzel." A even squeezed into words like *jealous* without making a sound, just to show off.

Z didn't show off. Neither did Y. In fact, Y didn't even mind being called both a consonant and a vowel.

"Come on, Y. Let's go to the front," Z said.

"Why?"

"Because it's boring at the end, and X is always cross."

"Excuse me," Z said to A, B, and C. "We want to go first."
"Okay," A said. "Go first."
It seemed too easy. Z looked at Y, who shrugged.
"You go first," A said again. "We'll sing as you go! *A, B, C—*"

Z and Y ran right into D, who blocked the way with his belly.
"Sorry, little letters. Can't get past me!"
"Why?" asked Y.
"I ate a dozen delicious doughnuts."
"I'll give you a baker's dozen if you let us through," Z said.
Greedy D agreed.

E stretched into a fence. “You can’t get past me. I’m the most important letter in the alphabet. And quite flexible, too.”

“Why?” asked Y.

“Everyone uses the letter E.”

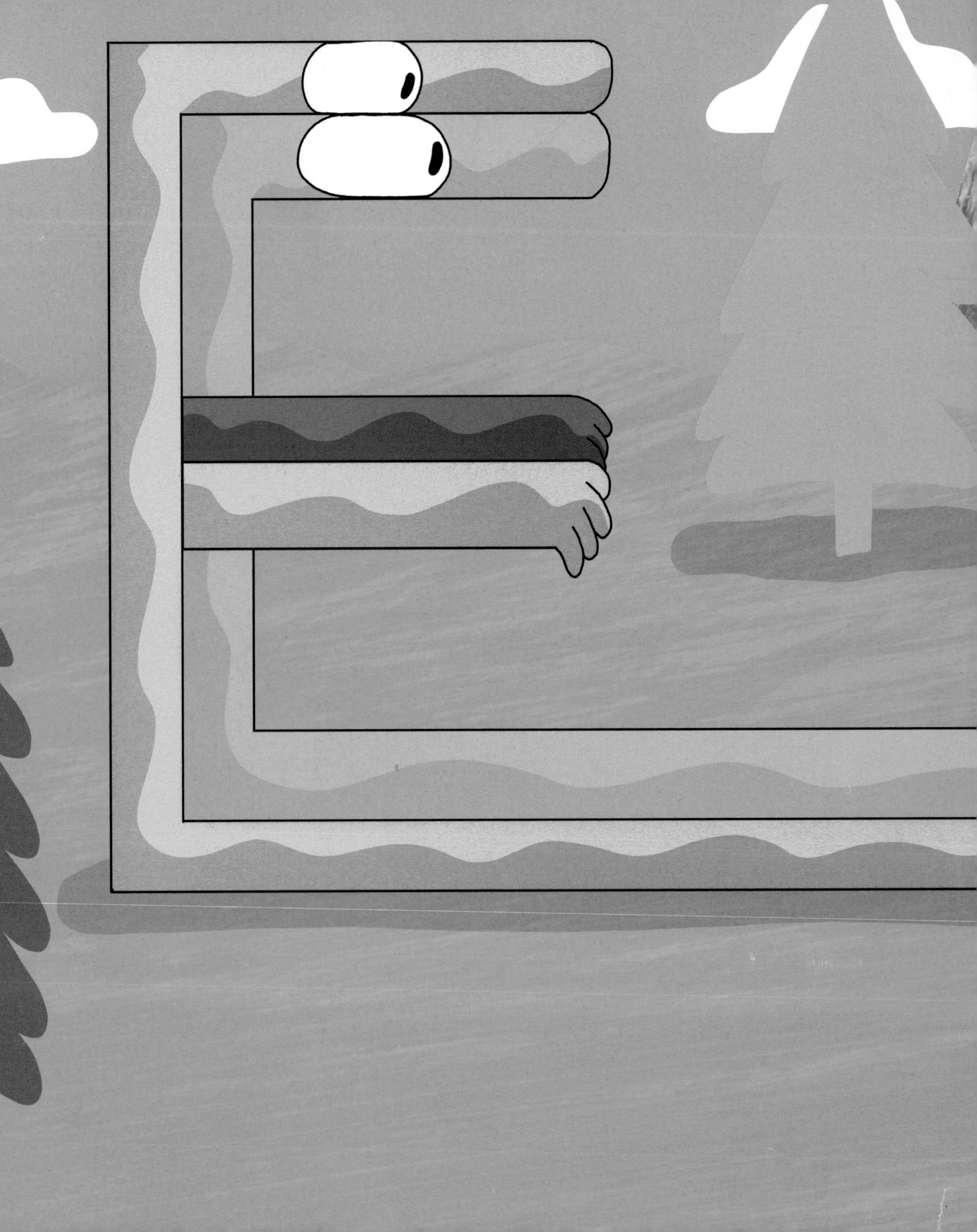

Z scratched her chin. "I think I know a really long word that doesn't need you."

"Try me," said E. "Even *me* needs me."

"How about *floccinaucinihilipilification*?" said Z.

E's eyes grew wide. "EEEEEEEEE!" he shouted.

F and G let Z and Y pass, after a warning.
“H can be a bit fussy,” F said.
“And grumpy,” G said.

When Z said they were going first, H sighed a heavy sigh. "Hhhhhhhhhhhhhh."

Z said, "Don't be so dramatic," and they kept going.

Z and Y hurried by I, who gazed into a mirror.
"*I* am incredible. *I* am inspiring. *I* am—"

Wild laughter greeted them next. Z cleared her throat.
"Can we help you?" J and K asked with sly smiles.
"We need to get through," Z said.
"I'm afraid that's not possible," said J.

"Why?" asked Y.
"The rest of the alphabet has been erased!" said K.
"What?" Z gasped.
"JUST KIDDING!" J and K burst into laughter.

LMNOP stuck together as if they formed their own word.

"Why are you two letters in the middle of the alphabet?"

"Why not?" asked Y.

L looked at M, who looked at N, who looked at O, who looked at P.

Y and Z snuck past while LMNOP tried to think of an answer.

Q was quick to stick out a leg, trying to trip up Z and Y. The two letters jumped over.

"Tell U that I said hello!" Q called after them.

R and S didn't understand why Z didn't like being at the end.
"We're at the end all the time," they said. "R makes things better. S gives things mass. It's not so bad."
Z disagreed and continued to T.

T stood tall and proud. "I'm Mr. T. Where are you two little troublemakers off to in such a tizzy?"

"We're going first," Z said.

"Ah, I go first a lot. Ever heard of *the*? It always goes first, and I go first with it."

"Great," Z said. "Now get out of *the* way."

U, V, and W didn't notice Z and Y.

"Two U's are better than one," teased W.

"Are not!" shouted U. "Just ask Q."

"Calm down!" V cried, holding them apart. "You're both very valuable to me."

Finally, Z and Y reached X, who crossed his arms and huffed.

"I can't believe you left me at the end!"

“You didn’t want to come anyway,” Z said. She knew X was always the letter to say, “Don’t do this!” or “Don’t touch that!”

“Fine,” X said. “At least the pirates appreciate me.”

ABC
Y

“We did it,” Z said. “We went first!”

Z and Y looked around. Somehow they were at the end again. The song echoed through the air, “—*Y and Z*!”

“Come on, Y. Let’s go to the front.”

ZYXW
RQPO
IHGFE